HOWLS IN THE NIGHT

TABLE OF CONTENTS

Credits

Written by Colin McComb
Edited by Dave Gross
Project Coordination by Andria Hayday and Harold Johnson
Cover Art by Paul Jaquays
Black and White Art by Mark Nelson
Graphics Coordination by Sarah Feggestad
Art Coordination by Peggy Cooper
Cartography by David C. Sutherland III
Typesetting by Angelika Lokotz

Thanks to Thomas Reid, Bill Connors, John R. Rateliff, Bill Slavicsek, and especially David Wise.

TSR, Inc.
POB 756
Lake Geneva
WI 53147 U.S.A

9466

TSR Ltd.
120 Church End, Cherry Hinton
Cambridge CB1 3LB
United Kingdom

eside the Sea of Sorrows rests Mordent, its chalk cliffs rising high above the pounding surf. Scattered rocks lie tumbled at the base of the white walls. Above the cliffs sprawl green meadows and hills. Past these lurk the moors, their undulating expanses dotted by stone monoliths and treacherous bogs. Stunted trees cluster like old gossips, providing scant shelter against the cold sea winds. Mists are common, rising from the ground at day's end to obscure the moor. Hidden shapes writhe and twist within these fogs, strange lights glow briefly and wink out, and the mournful baying of hounds rises above the susurrus of the leaves and weeds. It is here that the curse of the Wescote family has taken root, and it is here that it will be resolved.

Howls in the Night is designed for four to six player characters (PCs) of 3rd to 5th level. The party should include one or more priests, and at least one character should have a magical weapon. However, the characters should not be overequipped with magic, or they may find their obstacles too easy. The adventure should challenge the characters, not allow them to mince every obstacle in their path. On the other hand, the Dungeon Master (DM) shouldn't hesitate to adjust the numbers or power of the monsters encountered if the party is suffering too many grievous defeats. Scaring the players without killing their characters is always the best option. The DM should let foolish or reckless heroes meet horrible dooms.

The Dungeon Master should read carefully through the entire adventure before beginning play. This enables the DM to be well prepared for unexpected party actions and to modify any portions of the adventure to fit the campaign. It is essential in this adventure, because *Howls in the Night* has been designed to have several different conclusions, based on one of four adventure histories.

Each of the alternate backgrounds provides a different way of looking at the tragedy that occurred in Mordent one century ago. Burton Wescote is either an evil man or just a lovelorn suitor; Ann Campbell is either an innocent victim or a scheming fiend. The DM must choose one of the four histories and stick to it for the course of the adventure. When the heroes approach the climax of the adventure, the DM's chosen history will determine the means by which the curse can be overcome.

The panels of this module's cover contain the maps for all the major encounter areas in the adventure. Note **Part II** and **Part IV** share one map, since these events occur in the same location. **Part II** encounters are keyed with the number one (1); encounters for **Part IV** are keyed using letters.

The Flavor of Ravenloft

The importance of fear and horror checks cannot be overstated. The atmosphere of Ravenloft is one of Gothic terror. The setting is one in which the heroes move through the world discovering more and more horrifying secrets, encountering more and more evil beings. While the heroes ultimately face and have the chance to overcome the evil, they should first be terrified by it. It is essential that the DM create a feeling of terror for the players throughout the adventure. If the players are willing to role-play their heroes' fears, the DM need not require fear or horror checks. On the other hand, if they are unaffected by horrific occurrences, the whole adventure suffers. The DM is then perfectly justified in requiring fear or horror checks. Calling for the checks is thus purely a discretionary matter on the DM's part.

About Mordent

Mordent, the domain in which this adventure takes place, is a land of moors and hills, forests and downs, a country alternately bleak and beautiful. Farms dot the land, though most are clustered around Mordentshire, where the townsfolk band together against the darkness. They know that evil walks at night, for the land is full of supernatural horrors. Mordentshire is set in the western region of the Core.

This domain is under the purview of Lord Godefroy, a ghost residing in the capital of Mordentshire. Godefroy takes little interest in the lands beyond Mordentshire—or, indeed, in those lands beyond the borders of his haunted estate of Gryphon Hill. As lord of the domain, however, Godefroy is aware of most of the activities in his land; he simply does not take direct action in most cases. He certainly does not take part in this adventure, so the heroes need not worry about encountering a foe they cannot possibly defeat.

Mordentshire is the only notable settlement in the domain. However, there are many small fishing villages along the coast, as well as tiny villages scattered among the forests. The people are of every size and color, but there are no demihumans. The people are laborers, peasants, shepherds, and—most of all—fisherfolk. Fishing is the lifeblood of Mordent's natives, and most reserve their respect for someone who knows something of the sea.

Although they are polite, the people are extremely reserved around outsiders. They volunteer no information and do their best to keep to themselves. They are adroit at changing any subject about which they don't wish to speak—and they won't speak about most of the supernatural goings-on in the domain, believing that to speak of evil is to invite its presence.

The fisher folk are fairly superstitious, and for good reason. They have lived in a land of supernatural horrors, though it is a rare person who has actually witnessed any physical manifestation of the undead. The natives accept demihumans only warily, seeing them as a part of the supernatural world.

To the north and east of Mordentshire, about an hour's ride away, lies Wescote Manor. The short six miles, however, can seem endless. Thick woods press in on the furrowed path to the manor, giving way only to bleak and barren moors.

The Bare Facts

Although the heroes will most likely hear it from the Sheriff, anyone in Mordentshire can tell the following tale:

"About a hundred years ago, Burton Wescote and Ann Campbell were engaged to be married. It was an arranged wedding, valuable to both

families. There was no love lost between the Wescotes of Mordent and the Campbells of Dementlieu, but the groom, at least, was willing to go through with the marriage. Ann's family brought her to the manor so the couple could get acquainted before their union, though Ann remained vehemently opposed to the wedding. The rest of the Campbells stayed at the inn here in Mordentshire.

"Sometime during the night, Ann fled the manor into the bog, but not before killing Michael, one of the Wescote brothers, who apparently tried to prevent her from leaving. Burton set the dogs after her. Later, he said that he had trained them to subdue their prey and ordered them to do so when he loosed them. He and his dogs raced through the night after the fleeing Ann. The dogs outdistanced Wescote and gained ground on the girl. She fled into the mists that always seem to rise near the bog, the dogs close at her heels. Wescote ran after, a few minutes behind.

"Whatever happened out there, no one really knows.

"Wescote returned covered in mud and slime, his face scratched by brambles, and his clothes torn from where he had stumbled on his chase. They say he was crazy with fear . . . or loss. When questioned, he would say nothing of what had happened in the moors, except that Ann had died in the bogs and that he had had no hand in her death.

"Naturally, neither family believed him— Michael and Burton Wescote were known to be the closest of brothers, and everyone thought Burton had killed Ann in revenge. The Campbells thought it likely that Burton had chased Ann into the moors for the express purpose of killing her, but none could prove it. They moved back to Dementlieu, cursing the name of the Wescotes. The Wescotes praised Burton for pursuing the murderer to her death. The two families, who hadn't got along in the best of times, became bitter enemies.

"Then, for some reason or another, the Wescotes began disappearing, singly or in small

groups. Eventually, only a few ragged servants and the last of the Wescotes remained behind at Wescote Manor. One rumor holds that the Wescotes fled to re-establish their family someplace else, a place they could start afresh. Another rumor says that the Wescotes were killed by the great black Moor Hound, a dog said to be the embodiment of the Campbells' curse on the Wescotes.

"Regardless, the people of Mordentshire and the neighboring villages know better than to go out on the moors when the moon is high and the mist rises. The howls sound as soon as the sun sets, and only a fool would challenge the beast or beasts that make such cries. A few who have gone out seeking the lair of the creatures have found nothing, as though the monsters vanished during the daytime. Those who have sought the beasts in the night have been found in the morning at the edge of the moors with their entrails spilled about them. Needless to say, we pretty much leave the place alone these days."

Alternate Histories

The "bare facts" above represent common knowledge. This section reveals knowledge that is *not* so common. The DM must read through these histories to determine what background best suits the campaign. The skeleton of the history as outlined above remains the same, without casting guilt or blame on either the Wescotes or the Campbells.

One thing that remains constant, known by only a few, is the fact that it was not the "Campbell curse" that laid the Wescote family low. Or rather, it was not a curse given by the surviving Campbells: The curse was laid by Ann Campbell as she and the hounds were caught and sank in a pool of quicksand. As she descended deeper into the quagmire, Ann cried, "Bog take your bones and keep them, Burton Wescote! The hounds are forever yours." And here she forced another dog below the quicksand. "But now they lie beneath *my* hand!" She laughed bitterly in spite of her impending doom. "Live long and *suffer*, you selfish—" Then she sank below the surface. A few minutes later, bubbles rose to release Ann's final breath, and no more was ever seen of her.

And the rest, as they say, was history. Burton's relatives abandoned him, either through their own agency or through their deaths, leaving him to tend the house on the moor with only a few servants to aid him. Whether the curse or the fear of the curse drove this family away, none can say. However, no one doubts the efficacy of the curse, real or imagined.

Below are the four possible histories of Burton Wescote and Ann Campbell. They are each simple variations on the same basic tale, but the changes from one to another determine who will threaten the heroes and who will need their help.

History #1: Wescote the Scoundrel

In this history, Burton Wescote is a scoundrel and a rogue, a man of such bad character that Ann Campbell could not bear the thought of marrying him. When she attempted to flee, Burton's brother, Michael saw her and chased her through the halls. Cornered in the kitchen, she seized a knife to defend herself. In the midst of the struggle that followed Michael inadvertently thrust himself upon the blade and died. Ann fled into the night.

Enraged both by her flight and the death of his brother, the wicked Burton Wescote set loose his hounds. They hunted and finally caught Ann in the bog, driving her into the quicksand. Burton stood by and watched her drown, laughing when she pronounced her dying curse. To hide his evil deeds, he scratched himself with thorns, ripped his clothing and smeared it with mud, and then crawled home to present his story.

History #2: Ann the Shrew

On the eve of her wedding, the black-hearted Ann Campbell sought to exact some measure of vengeance on the man who had forced this marriage on her. Since she knew he doted on the dogs, she planned to slip out, slit the throats

of his favorite hounds, and head north to Port-a-Lucine in Dementlieu.

As she was selecting the knife for her crime, Michael Wescote encontered her in the kitchen. He saw the knife in her hand and feared she meant to harm his brother. The two struggled briefly, then Michael staggered away with the knife protruding from his chest.

Though black-hearted, Ann was horrified; she had never killed a person before, and she feared that her life would be short and miserable if she were caught by the Wescotes. Thus she chose to flee into the moors, leaving Burton to find his dying brother.

Outraged, Wescote set his dogs lose to hunt Ann Campbell and ran after them. But disaster also ran beside him.

When he arrived at the place where his pack howled and snarled, he saw that he was too late to bring Ann to justice. Though he cast about in vain for a branch or vine with which to save her from the quicksand, she cursed him and his family, and sank to her death.

Filled with grief for his brother, Burton staggered home across the moor, ignoring the cuts the thorns and jagged rocks inflicted on him. Through some miracle, he returned home safely, little knowing that his bad fortune was just beginning.

History #3: Evil Loathes Company

Burton Wescote had always been a black-hearted man, his mind always set on how best to reap a profit for himself from the misery of others. His proudest achievement, or so he thought at the time, was to arrange a marriage with Ann Campbell, thus putting the wealth of the Campbells at his disposal. Unfortunately, he didn't know that Ann was at least as evil as he, if not more. When they met, it was hate at first sight.

Burton was willing to endure a few months of marriage before killing Ann; he needed at least that long to get his hands into the Campbell treasury. Thus, he hid his disdain for the woman as best he could. However, she felt no such restraint. She declared to both families that she would rather die than be forced to marry "that Wescote cur."

Ignoring the enraged murmurs of his family, Burton smiled graciously and took the insults. Inwardly, he seethed, but his face betrayed none of the hatred in his heart.

When at last her family had left in the mistaken hope that perhaps she might be won over by the socially influential Wescote, Ann was escorted to her room by Wescote. Still smiling, he told her that any attempts to flee would be met with the *harshest* of punishment. So saying, he locked her in the room and headed downstairs to carouse with his family and friends.

Having had some experience at removing troublesome locks, Ann quickly escaped the room and headed downstairs. She went to the kitchen to select a knife for herself, imagining that she could greet Wescote in his room if he came up in a drunken stupor. Unfortunately, Michael Wescote entered just as she plucked the largest knife from the rack. Thinking him to be his brother, Ann plunged the knife into Michael before he could raise the alarm. She watched as he staggered back out of the kitchen, and she realized that he was going to fall right in the midst of Wescote and his cronies. She turned and fled the house.

Burton Wescote was outraged to see his plans destroyed by a headstrong girl. Enraged not so much by the death of his brother as by the fact that she was foiling his plans, Burton set his hounds after Ann and fetched a length of rope with which to bind her. Loping after the howling pack, he was soon outdistanced. Nevertheless, he followed the baying of the hounds.

When Ann's flight trapped her in the mire and saw him approaching, she cursed him loudly even as she fought off the dogs. He stood at the edge of the quicksand and chuckled over her plight. He then offered her a choice: marry him or perish in the quicksand. She spat at him, and in return, he threw the entire length of rope into the mire to sink with her. Burton stood and watched as both she and the rope vanished from

sight. The only unhappy aspect of the whole affair was that his dogs perished in the quicksand as well.

On the way home, he paused to make himself the perfect picture of the grieving groom. He slathered himself in mud, scratched himself with thistles, and contemplated ways to turn this situation to his advantage with the Campbells. Unfortunately, all his plans came to naught as the Campbells blamed him anyway.

History #4: Curse of the Bog

Burton Wescote never meant anyone any harm, but even he could see the disdain in Ann Campbell's eyes when she was brought to him for the arranged marriage. Neither of them had asked for the marriage, but Burton was resigned to it. Ann was not. Although she was good-hearted, she was blind to Wescote's virtues. She had been raised to believe that the Wescotes were evil monsters, and her family's acceptance of his proposal confused her.

The wedding night, she decided to flee. She paused to gather supplies for her journey to Mordentshire. Michael Wescote discovered her in the kitchen as she was holding a knife. Frightened, she struggled to get away and in the heat of the moment flailed at him stabbing him with the knife. Horrified by what she had done, Ann fled at once.

Burton, outraged at his brother's murder, set his hounds after Ann so that she could be brought to justice. The hounds were overzealous, however, and forced Ann into the mire. Burton arrived breathless and did his best to rescue her from the quicksand. Despite his efforts, Ann cursed him as she sank into the quicksand. When Burton returned to the manor, he found all in chaos. Afterwards, his family's fortune rapidly dwindled.

The Curse

The curse laid on Burton Wescote has five parts. The first brings the bogs of the moor closer to Wescote Manor year by year, until the area has nearly reached the keep. The manor is encircled by the bogs, and it is only through careful navigation that one can find a way through the mazes of fetid water and marshy land. In a few years, the manor house will sink into the bog, leaving only a small patch of land on which Wescote can live, and probably not for long there, given the likely fatality of the rest of the curse.

The second part creates the "bog hounds," supernatural creatures of mud and straw. These are the spiritual remnants of the hounds that pursued Ann Campbell into the quagmire. Linked by their shared deaths, the hounds follow Ann's bidding implicitly. Unlike the original pack, however, these hounds are limitless as long as Ann has the will to create them. For more information regarding the bog hounds, see the MONSTROUS COMPENDIUM® (MC) Appendix entry at the back of this book. The DM should become very familiar with these creatures.

The third part is embodied by the Moor Hound, the leader of the bog hounds once they have been created. The Moor Hound's sole mission, it seems, is to harry and vex Wescote at night until it can lure him into the swampy land to kill him. For more details, see the Appendix and the MC entry at the back of the book.

The fourth part has granted a horrid undead existence to Ann Campbell, making her spirit and mind the central force behind the evil of the bog. Whatever goodness might have lingered in her spirit has been destroyed by this mockery of a life. Now she seeks revenge on the man she blames for her demise. Her thirst for vengeance and her hatred are so great that she may live on even after all the conditions of the curse are fulfilled, playing havoc on unwary travelers. She hates all true life in general and wealthy men in particular, and she will seek to doom them as she has been doomed.

The fifth part grants Wescote immortality—at a price. He has lived more than a century, seemingly without aging. The reason behind this tortures him day and night, both physically and spiritually. In order to sustain his youthful form (and what good is immortality without the vigor to enjoy it?), he must venture into the moor daily and drink a cup of water from any of the bogs. Since the essence of Ann Campbell has spread through the nearby moor, he must, in short, drink of Ann to stay alive. This is not without its price. The water is mildly poisonous, inflicting stomach pains and nausea for 1d6 hours after imbibing it. All attacks and saving throws are made at –3 while under the influence of the bog water. The mere sight or smell of food or drink is enough to make one violently ill.

Yet Wescote has no choice but to continue consuming it. If he does not, he ages 10 years for every day that he tries to remain free of its nauseating influence. No matter how old he grows in outward appearance, he stays miserably alive. Once he tried to resist the effects of the pain, but he grew so old that the agony was unbearable. In his miserable state, he crawled to the bog, dragging his decrepit form behind him. He has no wish to endure such torment again. The lost years return to him at the rate of 10 years every two days.

The curse can be broken in several ways. First, the manor house can be destroyed, thus laying the history of the Wescotes to rest. Second, Ann Campbell's body can be dredged up from the muck of the bog and exposed to the light of the day. Third, the Moor Hound can be exposed to sunlight and destroyed; this does not actually break the curse, but it weakens the power Campbell holds. Finally, the heroes may throw Wescote into the mire, sending him to join the woman he killed a century ago.

Plot Overview

This section provides a synopsis of how the adventure is likely to play. Keep in mind that this synopsis is not the only order for this adventure, for gamers are unpredictable.

Each party follows its own priorities as they unravel the clues of the adventure.

Don't worry if the players surprise you with their choices. You should be able to get things back on track without obvious manipulation, permitting the players to investigate those things they think are important. Each clue they find should steer them back to the main adventure. And always feel free to improvise using the cast of non-player characters. Create more details and personality for these characters. Use NPCs to lead the party back to the correct path—or to lead them astray if the players are having too easy a time in the adventure. As always, play this adventure in your own style, and it will work best.

First, the heroes must arrive in Mordent. Then, while sheltering at an inn on the edge of Mordentshire or one of the tiny outlying villages, they hear the sound of hounds baying. The village folk explain that the dogs have been plaguing the village for years, and they plead

with the heroes to end the dogs' reign of terror. They send the heroes out onto the moor. While the heroes wander there, they find the bog area and from there are driven toward Wescote Manor by the dogs—or become lost until they encounter the manor.

Once inside Wescote Manor, they find Burton Wescote preparing a defense against the dogs, who pad around the manor restlessly. Burton explains his plight and paints himself as the innocent of the story, even if this is not truly the case. He asks the heroes to help break the curse so he can continue with a normal life.

Ideally, the heroes accept this offer. If they do, Wescote sends them into the bog to seek out the lost body of Ann Campbell. If they do not, Wescote tries to sweeten the deal with money. If all this fails, he simply curses them for cowards as they leave.

While in the bog, a mist rolls over the moors, hiding the sun. The heroes have several encounters that lead them closer to Campbell's body, but they are eventually driven to the manor. Here, they learn the truth about what happened long ago, as well as the nature of the curse—just in time to repel an attack from the bog hounds, led by the Moor Hound. From here, they can figure out a method to break the curse and travel on to their next adventure.

This is only the *most likely* course of events. There is always the chance that the heroes will go chasing off on a false trail or abandon the adventure entirely, especially if Wescote is revealed to be a villain.

The DM will want to prevent the players from avoiding the entire adventure. Though the players might choose to ignore the adventure here, there is nothing to say that they cannot be cursed until they perform a deed to rectify their ambivalence. Perhaps, as they traipse away across the moors, they hear the lonely howling of a large hound. Thereafter, when the party attempts to hide or move by stealth, the howling sets in again, rising in intensity until not even the dullest guard could mistake it and fail to be alert. In short, this curse badgers the heroes when they least need or want it, destroying fragile plans where applicable.

If nothing of this nature suggests itself, the heroes' horses might be mauled by a giant dog in the night, though the party never gets a glimpse of the beast responsible. If they post a watch, the guard slips into a light doze, awaking to the sounds of thrashing, screaming horses. Or, at an inn, the heroes could wake to feel hot breath on their faces, but when they open their eyes, there is nothing there. Closer inspection, however, reveals that some large dog has been in the room with them, for it has tracked muddy footprints and drool all over the room, as well as the other rooms of the inn. One of the few remedies that the heroes may discover can help the heroes resolve their minor curse, through a wandering seer, is that they must return to help Burton Wescote.

This solution may be extended to other adventures in Ravenloft. When the characters fail to fulfill some obligation that they have taken upon themselves or—more likely—if they neglect some duty, they can be marked in some way by that adventure. This mark should reflect the nature of the quest they have abandoned, but rarely should it overwhelm the heroes with memories of quests forgotten. These minor hauntings may take many forms: scars that do not fully heal; incessant headaches, made worse whenever the heroes view scenes that remind them of their neglected duty; ominous fortunes told by wandering Vistani; recurring nightmares which prevent spellcasters from memorizing all their spells; or even a real mark upon the heroes' faces, causing all strangers to view them as outcasts. Any mark should serve as a reminder of inaction more than as punishment. Use them to spur the players to action, but not to destroy the heroes.

Welcome once again to Ravenloft. Mordentshire's little homes huddle against the chill night. The distant surf, mingled with the calls of hounds, warns even as it beckons. The moon is bright among the clouds, and even now the mists roll slowly in from the moors. . . .

I n this first section, the heroes arrive at Mordentshire and learn of the hounds that terrorize the town before facing the bog hounds themselves. The party can begin the adventure either inside the Demiplane of Dread or in their own world. If the heroes begin outside the Misty Borders, it is a simple matter to bring them to Mordentshire. The DM can simply read or paraphrase the following text, modifying it where necessary to fit into the ongoing campaign.

> As you trudge down the road, the land is cast in shadow as thick clouds veil the setting sun. A chill wind rises suddenly, blowing in your face, chafing with its force. In minutes, the sun is entirely hidden, and the countryside is plunged into darkness. The wind rises in a lonely canine howl . . . then dies. Just as abruptly as it began, the night falls still, not a breath of a breeze.
>
> After a bit, the rising moon peeks through the veil of clouds, but a mantle of mist rises from the damp ground beside the road. With preternatural speed, the fog thickens into a cottony gray obscuring sight beyond 20 feet. Sounds are likewise muffled in the thick mists.
>
> As the minutes pass, the fog thins and then dissipates, revealing an unfamiliar land from the one you saw before the fog!
>
> Dozens of yards ahead, past the flanking farmlands, you can see the lights of a town gleaming through the night. Beyond the town, comes the sound of waves crashing upon a rocky shoreline.

If the heroes are already in Ravenloft but nowhere near Mordentshire, the Mists transport them to the town as described above. If the heroes are in the vicinity, they find that their road takes some unexpected twists leading them to the town. Regardless, the heroes find themselves entering Mordentshire at night, or just as the sun is setting and people are hurrying home.

These folk all seem to be fishers, farmers, or the spouses of those who toil on land or sea. They are rough, weather-bitten people who have no time to waste. The locals give the heroes glances of mild curiosity, but none stop to ask the heroes what they are doing in this town since the locals are intent on getting home before the deep of the night. If there are demi-humans with the party, the village people simply give the party a wider berth, steering clear to make sure of avoiding contact with the group.

The people of the town talk to the party if the heroes can catch their attention. The people are friendly, if somewhat rough around the edges, and they can tell the heroes general information about the town, as well as the name of the local inn most likely to welcome adventuring types: The Beached Mermaid. The rest of the town offers services one might expect from a town of 2,000, including a blacksmith with no great talent, several taverns, a general store, and more. The people of the town keep mostly to themselves, preferring not to socialize with the heroes.

The Beached Mermaid

T he tavern is an island of warmth amid the autumn breeze blowing off the sea. Dressed in mahogany and brass, the whole bar has a nautical decor. A roaring blaze in the fireplace dispels the chill of the night. The patrons of the bar are, for the most part, grizzled sea-faring types. All 15 of them glance up briefly as the heroes enter, then turn back to their business almost immediately.

The innkeeper is a white-haired, bushy-bearded bear of a man named Captain Garrett Nancy. The Captain, as he prefers to be called, serves the heroes with a smile. He hovers nearby to speak with them. As a non-native to Mordent, the Captain finds that the townsfolk do not speak to him as much as he would like, and he certainly enjoys hearing tales of the outside world. Indeed, if the heroes can tell him some interesting news, he buys them the first round of drinks. Even if they don't, he settles down to swap stories with the party, recognizing in them kindred spirits filled with wanderlust.

If the heroes are looking for a place to spend the night, he can offer them some clean rooms for a mere 5 sp per person. Supper costs 1 gp.

As the heroes settle down to enjoy the evening, a few more people arrive. The Captain then closes and bars the door. He gives the heroes a wan smile as he does so, telling them, "The night ain't safe".

After a short time, he returns to their table and says:

"Mayhap, barring a door at night seems a bit queer to you. Let me tell you why I do it.

"Here in Mordentshire the night is full of strange things. The house on Gryphon Hill . . . well, that's only one of the places that's said to be haunted. Still, as they say around here, if you don't bother evil, it won't bother you. But all that's begun to change recently. Do you hear that howling?"

Above the moan of the wind, you can hear the sound of dogs baying. The sound is faint, but sends shivers along your spine.

"Aye, those hounds prowl the countryside at night in Mordentshire. They haven't worked up the gumption to come down into the town, but they've been harrying the outlying farms, killing those who wander abroad in the night and making everyone afraid to travel after sunset. The strange thing is that they never come out during the day—nobody's ever seen one in the sunlight.

"What this town needs is someone to get rid of those dogs. Everyone here would gladly reach into their purses to raise the money for bounty hunters to get rid of those beasts.

"Now you . . . you seem more daring than the rest of the folks hereabout; better suited for danger, if I read you aright. You interested?"

Simply by passing a bowl among those at the inn—all of whom look like they're ready to spend the night here rather than wander out into the darkness—the Captain gathers a bounty pot of 100 gp, surely enough to persuade someone to take on a pack of hungry dogs. If this is not enough for the party, the Captain promises to check with the Mayor the next day to try to get the town to throw some money into the pot to sweeten the deal.

If the heroes are eager to leave in the night to hunt the hounds, the Captain won't unbar the door during the night. But he will offer the heroes room and board for the night, as well as breakfast, to ensure that they can begin their hunt well fed and rested. If the party insists on heading out this night, they will find a hostile crowd of locals barring their way. If the heroes sneak out during the night, proceed to **Part II**, changing references from the day to the night, and have the heroes encounter the Sheriff and his men near the bog.

If the heroes decide to sleep, their dreams are plagued by an enormous black mastiff, a dog larger and fiercer than any they have ever seen. Tell any player who asks about the dream that the vision of this dog is no doubt caused by the incessant howling of the hounds in the night. Then smile as if you know better.

The next day, the weather is full of foul portent. During the night, a thick fog has rolled in off the ocean, pressing against the windows of the inn as if eager to enter. The embers of last night's fire still warm the now empty common room. Those who spent the night have left to get at the day's work.

True to his word, the Captain has a fine breakfast spread out for the heroes.

After the heroes have eaten their fill and shoved their plates away, a boy bursts in the inn's door. Panting and out of breath, he shouts, *"Shepherd Dawson's been killed!"*

The Hunt

The local Sheriff and some of his deputies arrive close on the lad's heels. A crowd of people begins to gather outside. The Sheriff eyes the heroes and the innkeeper, and declares, *"The mayor has authorized me to deputize all the able-bodied folk of the village to put an end to these hounds. We're going to search out these dogs' lair. They've killed one of the shepherds, and he'll be the last to die if I have any say in the matter."*

The Sheriff is not looking for arguments. He will reply to any questions the heroes might have about the case. He doesn't have many answers though, and he will not take much time to satisfy the party's curiosity. After all, he does have a hunt to organize. He knows that the dogs have become bolder, entering the fields around the very town, and that they claimed their first victim last night. He has not yet been out to examine the body, as he began organizing this search party as soon as he heard of the atrocity.

He also knows the lay of the land. He tells the heroes to follow him, and heads out the door. If the party does not comply, the Sheriff at first tries to reason with them. Failing that, he then tells them that he'll have them thrown in jail if they cannot find it in themselves to do the decent thing and come to the aid of the town. He is perfectly serious in this threat and will have the party bound by the mass of people outside, their equipment confiscated until they decide to aid the town.

The Sheriff is initially polite, but the reports of the day are already wearing on his nerves, and he does not want more trouble on his hands.

When the heroes accept, the Sheriff leads the group of deputies, about 100 strong, toward the shepherd's house. All of the townsfolk are strangely quiet. The Sheriff invites the heroes to walk with him. As they walk through the fog, the heroes can question him about the land. The Sheriff is amiable, though clearly upset about the killings. He can tell them the story of Burton Wescote ("The Bare Facts" from the Introduction), as well as any rumors, clues, or red herrings you wish to give the players. The Sheriff tells the heroes that the Wescote manor house is a few miles to the northeast, but the hunt shouldn't take them that far.

Eventually, the hunters arrive at the site of Shepherd Dawson's cottage. It is a ramshackle little place, badly weathered by the harsh climate of the area. The building is secure, and holds no clues within as to what might have killed the shepherd. Around the back of the building are the sheep pens, which are strangely silent. Once the characters round the cottage, they can see why.

Every single sheep has had its throat torn out. Lying in the middle of the pen is the body of a middle-aged man.

> "Someone's got a morbid sense of humor," the Sheriff says. He gestures toward the body of the shepherd. The man's throat has been torn open by some creature, jagged tears surround the wound. Standing over the corpse is a straw sculpture of a dog, a large hound patched together with mud. There is blood dripping from the thorny teeth of the figure. As you look, an icy blast of wind blows the beast apart, scattering the straw and leaving only a few bloodstained stalks of hay to mark where it once stood.

If the heroes check for tracks, they find something rather odd. Both the hound's and shepherd's prints clearly lead to this spot, but there are no other prints to indicate that the statue was placed there by a third party. If the heroes do not check this obvious clue, one of the other deputies points it out to them. The Sheriff is befuddled by this once it is pointed out, but he takes charge quickly. He divides the hunting party into groups no larger than eight people. He then tells each group to form a line. He assigns the heroes to follow the tracks back to their source, and tells the others to fan out in an effort to pick up other tracks.

The trail the heroes are to follow heads northeast toward the Wescote manor. The Sheriff remarks upon this, saying, *"Perhaps they live in the bog near the manor."* His manner is uneasy, and he looks about the area as if he were expecting an attack at any time. "I wish this blasted fog would clear. It was gone for a short time this morning, but it's really come back with a vengeance. It'll make tracking harder. We're going to have to have a system to keep track of each other. Any suggestions?"

The Sheriff gives the heroes an opportunity to suggest some method of communication. If no one suggests anything, the Captain suggests that they call out every few minutes so that no one gets lost. Using a rope will only permit one group of eight to be tied together.

Once the method has been agreed upon, the hunt sets out. It is a good thing the Sheriff insisted on communication, for visibility out here is limited to about 20 feet. The heroes cannot even make out the group next to theirs, but the communication flows well, with shouts coming up and down the line every few minutes. Still, the whole hunting party is spreading out, becoming more and more dispersed.

Suddenly, a mournful yowling rises. It sounds as if scores of dogs are howling in unison. The eerie sound of the dogs grows louder as the sounds of the other hunting party groups diminishes. Suddenly there are screams of pain and surprise in the distance, as well as the bays of hunting dogs. It sounds as though another group of the deputies is being attacked!

If the heroes go to investigate, they find that the fog has confused their sense of direction,

muffling the sound and making it seem as though it comes from someplace entirely different. Once the heroes go to the aid of the rest of deputies, they find themselves wending their way deeper and deeper into the bog, drawn closer to a meeting with Burton Wescote. No matter which way they go, the fog confuses them and leads them toward the manor.

If the heroes opt not to go to the aid of the rest of the hunting party, or if they stay in place, they are hunted by a pack of bog hounds that pick up their scent. The heroes become aware that they are being hunted when howls sound nearby, seemingly within 30 feet. However, because of the density of the fog, the heroes can see nothing. Sound carries well, though it reveals nothing of the direction of the source, and the heroes can hear the panting of several hounds and the padding of their feet.

Once the hounds have surrounded the heroes, they fall silent and close in, baying suddenly only when the heroes can see them. The heroes and other characters may be required to make fear checks when they see the eyeless dogs looming out of the fog.

Bog Hounds (10): Int Semi; AL NE; AC 5; MV 15; HD 2+2; hp 16 each; THAC0 19; #AT 3; Dmg 1–4/1–4/1–6; SZ M; ML 15; XP 65 each.

The hounds fight to the death; they have no life for which to be careful. When they are destroyed, they revert to the mud and straw from which they were formed; the mist that provides them life drifts away unseen in the thick fog. Again, the heroes may be have to make a fear check when the creatures die and transform to straw and muck. This is a one-time check, for the heroes will become acclimated to this after they have faced the creatures once.

During the battle, the hounds force the heroes toward the bog. Proceed to **Part II: Bog Take Your Bones.**

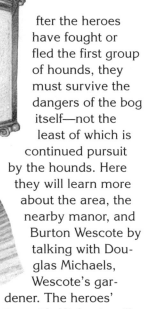

After the heroes have fought or fled the first group of hounds, they must survive the dangers of the bog itself—not the least of which is continued pursuit by the hounds. Here they will learn more about the area, the nearby manor, and Burton Wescote by talking with Douglas Michaels, Wescote's gardener. The heroes' interaction with Michaels will determine the reception they receive when they finally arrive at Wescote Manor.

Hounded!

The sounds of the other deputies have faded to nothing during the battle. Your surroundings are damp and marshy, the sound of water dripping off moss draped skeletons of trees fills the lonely moor. All around rises the drone of buzzing insects and the harsh cawing of carrion birds. The sounds seem somehow lost and forlorn through the dense fog.

Then out of the lonely gray comes the baying of the dread hounds as the pack once more takes up the hunt, and you must turn and flee deeper into the depths of the great bog. Your haphazard flight leads into thicker growths, green, yet rancid, somehow drawing strength from the stagnant waters, through which you slog. Abruptly your foot sinks into a morass! Only quick reflexes save you from being swallowed by the bog, as you come to realize this entire swamp hides danger everywhere and a misstep could spell your doom!

The heroes will be pursued by the bog hounds while they remain on the moors. The heroes will not have time to stop and investigate, for as soon as they dispatch their attackers, four more hounds take up the hunt. The heroes have ten minutes (rounds) at most between attacks. Inexorably, the heroes will be driven toward the lost Douglas Michaels, Burton Wescote's gardener. But before they encounter him, they must learn how to navigate the bog.

The heroes first must deal with slowed movement. Unless they have some magic that allows them unrestricted action in this plant-choked place, their movement rate is reduced to 1/3 of normal. Though there are game trails and small paths criss-crossing the entire bog, the trails are so overgrown that they hamper movement significantly. If the heroes are on one of the more established trails used by the hounds or the servants in Wescote Manor, then their movement rates rise to 2/3 normal.

The greatest danger of the bog is quicksand. There is a 15% chance each round that the heroes enncounter a patch of quicksand. The patch will be from 10 to 60 feet wide and may actually support their weight for a few rounds before the heroes realize their predicament. Each hero must then make a successful saving throw versus spell or step into the quicksand.

If anyone falls into the quicksand, they must each make a Swimming proficiency check. If they succeed, the victim can stay afloat indefinitely, though any movement thorough the morass is extremely difficult (1 foot every three rounds). Those who fail have panicked and are treated as if they do not have the Swimmiing proficiency at all.

Characters without the Swimming proficiency can stay afloat for one-quarter of their Constitution score, in turns. Each turn spent in the quicksand exhausts the heroes and gives them a cumulative –1 penalty to attacks until the heroes have rested at least one turn for each turn spent in the quicksand.

Once a victim sinks below the surface, he can survive only briefly. Given a good gulp of air,

heroes can hold their breath a number of rounds equal to 1/6 their Constitution score. After this time, if they continue to try to hold their breaths, they must make a successful Constitution check each round, with a cumulative –2 penalty after the first round. Once the check is failed, the character drowns.

Rescuing someone trapped in quicksand merely requires the rescuer to reach out with a branch, rope or other object, to find something to anchor themselves to on this marshy ground and to reel the victim in as he hangs on. A rescuer may jumps into the quicksand to save a drowning person, but must have the Swimming proficiency or else he will be in just as much jeopardy.

The safest way to travel in this bog is to rope together oneself together with one's companions. Though this causes a –1 to Hit penalty to each hero as well as limiting movement, it is far preferable to the alternative.

No matter their course or preparations, the party will encounter at least one group of bog hounds. These beasts will attack until they are outnumbered by 4 to one or greater, at which point the survivors will flee into the mist.

Bog Hounds (4): Int Semi; AL NE; AC 5; MV 15; HD 2+2; hp 13, 13, 10, 9; THAC0 19; #AT 3; Dmg 1–4/1–4/1–6; SZ M; ML 15; XP 65 each.

The party first hears the lost gardener thrashing through the underbrush after they dispatch the first group of bog hounds.

From around a bend in the game trail, comes a terrified horrified screaming and chorused by the baying of hounds who have cornered their prey. A stooped old man, bloodied and muddied, hobbles out of the undergrowth, the horrible, eyeless hounds close on his heels. His pitiful cries for help are weak and hoarse. The dogs, undaunted by this new foe, throw themselves into battle foaming and snarling.

These four hounds have the same statistics as the ones described above.

I. Meeting Michaels

Once the heroes have dispatched the beasts, the grateful man speaks:

"Thanks t' ye fer yer timely assistance. Without it, I'd surely be dead. But I'm gettin' ahead of meself. Allow me t' introduce meself to ye. I am Douglas Michaels, the gardener to Sir Burton Wescote, the owner of this property and the nearby manor. I was out here in the bog t' gather some herbs fer our Cook when I was set upon by the nasty dogs.

"I've got to say, I never expected to see anyone wanderin' through the bog of their own accord. Even during the daytime, when the hounds don't come out, this place is usually shunned by the locals. 'Course, I can see yer not locals, so that might explain it. Still, didn't anyone tell ye that this place is s'posed to cursed?

"Y' know, now't I think on't, this is th' first time I've ever seen these hounds during th' daytime. That's a powerful puzzle. It's supposed to be safe to go out in the light." an involuntary shivering shakes his frail frame.

"If you could be seein' me back t' the manor, we could look after those wounds and maybe arrange fer some dinner. What say ye?"

The sun pierces the fog soon after the heroes rescue the gardener. Michaels leads the way back to the manor, chatting all the way. If the heroes cannot think of anything to talk about, Michaels will talk about anything that comes to mind. These topics include the weather, his job, and the dilapidated state of the manor house.

If asked about Wescote and the curse, Michaels explains that he is devoted to Wescote—or more properly, he is devoted to his job. He might speak glowingly of the master, or he might whisper of the master's unpredictable temper, depending on the history chosen. If Wescote is evil, Michaels tells the heroes that, though he hates speaking ill of another,

Wescote is a man prone to violent rages and is sometimes an unreasonable master, though he always presents a civilized face to his guests. Michaels also begs the heroes not to tell anyone what he has said; he loves his job, if not his master, and would hate to have to look for another at this time in his life.

Michaels doesn't know much about the curse. However, he does know that the bog seems to have been creeping steadily closer to the manor in the fifty years that he has been working there. Also, strangely enough, the master never seems to get any older, as though he were being kept young by some supernatural agency.

He knows that the hounds are usually nocturnal creatures, and he stays inside at night. For this reason, he has never seen the apparition described in **Part III: The Hounds Are Forever Yours,** though he has heard of it from the other servants.

After 15 to 20 minutes of walking, Wescote Manor's silhouette can be seen dimly in the fog, its gabled roof rising above the treeline. Even from this distance, it seems more a derelict than an inhabited manor. As the heroes draw closer, they can see that the manor's windows are boarded up, the doors thick and stout. The building is badly in need of paint, a strange contrast to the well-kept grounds. The bog is held at bay only by the thick stone walls that ring the estate, though in places it looks as though the wall has crumbled under the steady onslaught of the marshy ground.

If the heroes ask why the manor house is boarded up, Michaels replies, "Ach, it's because o' them bog hounds, and their leader, the great Moor Hound. They've thrown themselves at the windows and forced their way through the doors more than once. 'Bout 40 years ago, after I'd been here a while, Master Wescote simply decided not t' go t' the trouble of replacin' the windows. Every night those dogs come at us and ruin whatever work I've done durin' the day. We got tired of puttin' the stuff back together. I hope ye'll fergive the mess."

ince the heroes aided Michaels, they are welcomed as honored guests, for Wescote has a difficult time recruiting new help since his reputation in Mordentshire is tarnished. Though no one from the town can reliably report whether Burton is alive or dead, the Wescote family is believed to be cursed. Only the least superstitious of the locals even consider hiring on at the family manor, leaving the manor with few candidates for employment.

Eventually, Wescote asks the heroes to help break the curse that has plagued him and his family. If the heroes agree to help, they can find several clues regarding the nature of the curse in the manor house itself.

The first clue is Wescote's own testimony. However, since even the dullest player is likely to realize that this version of the history is slanted, there are more clues. The servants may be questioned, and, if Wescote is evil, the heroes may see him beating one of them in a fit of rage. There is also the apparition of the night of the curse; Wescote himself shows the heroes the scene, but he hides his own involvement in it. The information the heroes gain should be enough to lead them into the bog, where they can learn more of the curse of the Wescotes.

Wescote Manor

The manor is a rambling, two-story building, filled with dust and antiques. Descriptions of the manor's rooms and any items of value follow the notes on the servants. The DM should feel free to add ordinary furniture and other items to these descriptions as the heroes explore. None of these furnishings should be especially attractive to a thief, but there is always the chance that a hero will try to filch a few things. Remind the players that they are guests if thier heroes begin filling their pockets. The few remaining servants have quarters on the first floor, but most may be encountered anywhere in the manor.

The Servants

Darrell Holmes (butler and 2nd-level fighter): AC 7; MV 12; hp ; S 13, D 12, C 14, I 13, W 14, Ch 11; #AT 1; Dmg 1–6; AL LN or LE; THAC0 19.

Darrell is polite and servile but not especially friendly. He remains in the servants' wing until he is summoned. Having been an adventurer once before, he has little admiration for the heroes. His personality otherwise mirrors Wescote's—if Wescote is evil, Holmes is haughty and cunning, brutal when he has the upper hand. If Wescote is good, Holmes is gentle, though still somewhat arrogant.

Martine Garrett (cook): AC 10; MV 12; hp 3; S 10, D 13, C 10, I 12, W 9, Ch 9; #AT 1; Dmg 1–4; AL N; THAC0 20.

Martine is officious and scheming, keenly conscious of the social hierarchy among the servants. She always wants to make herself appear better than the others, usually by criticizing other servants unfairly, or attributing her mistakes to another. She is an excellent cook, despite her character flaws.

Douglas Michaels (gardener) AC 9; MV 9; hp 4; S 14, D 15, C 13, I 10, W 13, Ch 8; #AT 1; Dmg 1–3; AL NG; THAC0 20.

Douglas is a gentle old man who has been in the service of the Wescote family longer than any of the other servants. He walks with a limp, having broken his leg badly years ago.

Gabrielle Morgan (maid): AC 10; MV 12; hp 3; S 8, D 12, C 15, I 9, W 12, Ch 13; #AT 1; Dmg 1–2; AL NG; THAC0 20.

Friendly and knowledgeable, Gabrielle keeps her keen mind hidden behind a facade of stupidity. She's the one who talks to the heroes about the apparition.

First Floor

Foyer: The entryway is graciously appointed, but appears in need of some new furniture. What remains looks as though it has been here for decades. A stairway leads to the second floor, where a balcony overlooks the foyer.

Living Room: This room has been abandoned. Broken glass litters the floor, and the door is nailed shut. Mud and straw from slain bog hounds are scattered about the floor. Several books have been torn from the shelves, their chewed pages scattered about the room. Because it is shut off from the rest of the manor, this room is distinctly cooler.

Drawing Room: Here are the wrapped gifts for the wedding that never happened. The room is full of silverware (worth 200 gp), a complete set of china dishes and plates (worth 500 gp), several pieces of art (including paintings, statuary, and a violin; each is worth 200 gp), weapons (including a *broad sword +1*), and a suit of plate armor. The armor is purely ornamental, but attractive (worth 400 gp).

Dining Room: The dining room is one of the rooms still in good repair. The mahogany furniture is polished to shine with a mellow glow, and the place settings are sparkling clean. One thing seems odd: there is a darker, bare spot on the wall where a painting obviously used to hang. Wescote says that it was a portrait of his grandfather that was damaged; in reality, it is a picture of himself, and it is hidden away in the basement.

Ballroom: Before the heroes can enter, they must pry boards and nails from the doors, as this room has been sealed shut. Once they are inside, the heroes can see that this once-beautiful room is now littered with hay and mud, all its tall elegant windows shattered. If the heroes ask Wescote or any of the servants about this disarray, they are told that the hounds once broke inside, so now the room has been abandoned. Like the living room, this chamber is decidedly cool. A balcony upstairs contains orchestral seating, with a railing running around the length of the ballroom.

Kitchen: The kitchen is well-kept and bright, with scrubbed pots and pans dangling from the ceiling. There is a large pantry and spice rack here, and a large food preparation area dominates the room.

Servants' Quarters: The servants' quarters are clean and well-kept. Each of the servants has his or her own room and keeps about 5 gp worth of valuables hidden away here.

Second Floor

Study: This room is securely locked (poor quality lock; +15% chance to open). It doubles as a library and a study. Lining the walls are books on history, art, and fiction. There is also a large section on the occult, specifically concentrating on works dealing with case studies of ghosts and curses. There are several books by the noteworthy Dr. Van Richten tucked into the shelves.

The room is comfortably appointed, with stuffed leather chairs, a large oak desk, and a huge fireplace. There is a couch facing the fire, a rumpled blanket lies across it attesting that someone has been sleeping by the fire. Paintings adorn the panelled walls, studies of the lords of Wescote Manor. The last painting, dated 100 years ago, depicts someone who looks remarkably like the current lord.

About the desk are scattered papers, each of

which is devoted to considering ways to break the curse Wescote lies under.

If Wescote is evil, he has written notes cursing Campbell here, containing sentiments like, "I should have killed her when I had the chance!" If the heroes enter the study, he'll try to prevent them from examining the desk, saying, "There's nothing of importance here. The key to the curse lies in the bog."

The words of the curse are engraved above the mantelpiece, next to a picture of a beautiful young lady, with auburn tresses, a full figure, a hawklike nose and piercing green eyes. This is so Wescote can study the curse in an effort to figure a way to break it. To date, he has not found one short of dying, which he would never consider a viable alternative. The curse reads:

"Bog take your bones
and keep them, Burton Wescote!
The hounds are forever yours,
but now they lie beneath my hand!
Live long and suffer, you selfish—"

A dagger sticks in the wall nearby, as if someone had hurled it in a fit of anger.

A safe behind one of the paintings contains a deed to the land, 500 gp, a collection of 15 gems worth 200 gp each, and a leather pouch holding 100 pp. The safe's lock is excellent (imposing a –20% penalty on any attempts to open it). It's key is in Wescote's room.

Master Bedroom: Wescote's bedroom is functional and free of the resplendent decor of the mansion of old. It contains a four-poster bed, a dresser, and a large closet. It contains no valuables, except a key to the safe in the study; it is in a drawer on a bedside table.

Gallery: The music gallery overlooks the ballroom. The mess of the ballroom below does not spread to up here, though the dust of the years covers the place. The area is little used.

Bedrooms: The bedrooms are sparse but comfortable. They contain only a bed, dresser, stool and closet.

Basement

The basement's ceiling is vaulted to support the weight of the house above. The ceiling is only about five feet high, requiring those who come down here to stoop for their tasks. The basement's only ornaments are cobwebs and dust, its only tenants spiders and rats.

Wine Cellar: This once-grand collection of rare wines has dwindled to fewer than two dozen bottles. Rarely has a servant been able to get to town to replenish it.

Equipment Room: This room is littered with rusty or damaged furnishings and riding equipment. It is apparent that none of this has been disturbed in the past year, judging by the dust on everything. Among the equipment, beneath an old canvas, is the painting removed from the dining room upstairs. If the heroes discover this and remove the protective canvas, they will find that it depicts someone who looks like their host, though oddly the painting itself is dated as many decades old.

The Course of Events

When the heroes enter the manor house, they are greeted warmly by Burton Wescote, an engaging, clever man. He listens attentively to the gardener's story, nodding sympathetically at all the right places. He seems genuinely pleased to have visitors in his house, and urges them to stay for dinner.

He summons the maid and the butler to tend to the party's injuries, sending them to one of the bedrooms on the second floor. When they have had their wounds washed and bandaged, Wescote sends for them. He leads them on a tour of his manor, showing them the rooms of interest.

By the time the tour ends, dinner is prepared. Wescote insists that the heroes stay for dinner. If they decline, Wescote tells them that he knows the source of the hounds and will reveal all over dinner. He is true to his word, telling them the story of the curse laid upon his family. However, no matter his involvement in the story, he makes sure he is portrayed as the innocent victim. He simply changes his involvement, using History #1 if #4 is true, and History #3 if #2 is true (see pages 5–8). *Detect lie* and other divination magics are useless here—the hero casting the spell receives no reading and knows it, rather than receiving a false reading altogether.

   After telling his story, Wescote insists that everyone come up to the study with him; he is eager to show them a sight. "However," he warns, "you had best be prepared to stay up late. What I wish to show you takes place in the early hours of the morning, so you might wish to have some sleep beforehand." He says no more about the matter, preferring to let the apparition speak for itself. Once in the study, he invites the heroes to make themselves comfortable; he seats himself at his desk and picks up one of his books on hauntings.

Time passes slowly till at last the clock strikes three. Wescote strides over to the large window. "Ah, it begins again," he murmurs. "Every night at three, her apparition forms and she takes her pack of hounds out to hunt the moors. Watch!"

   He gazes out on the expanse of land at the back of the house as a ghostly shimmer rises from the land. From your vantage point, you can see the glow shape itself into the form of a young woman, but you are too far away to make out the her face. You can tell that she gazes at the house for a moment, and then whirls and races off toward the waiting moor. Soon thereafter, a pack of ravenous hounds races after her.

   "There she goes with her dogs," Wescote murmurs, "off to hunt the innocents who wander abroad." He closes the drapes and fastens them quickly, but not before you glimpse another figure racing after the pack.

If asked about the second ghostly figure, Wescote says that he has never been able to discern the identity of the figure, that it has only recently joined the hunt. If the heroes pull aside the curtains, they are in time to see the figures disappear off into the moor, fading as they enter a small dale in the distance.

Once the phantom show has ended, Wescote turns to the party: "That's my curse. Can you help me? Will you seek out the vengeful spirit of Ann Campbell and lay her to rest, to bring me peace? I can outfit and feed you, and give you rough directions to where Ann died.

If the party agrees, Wescote crows, "Excellent! I'll have the maid show you to your rooms! You can start in the morning." He rings a small bell on his desk, and a few minutes later, a sleepy Gabrielle comes in to show the heroes to the guest rooms.

This phantom show repeats every night until the curse is broken. If the heroes wish to witness the phantom in its entirety (something Wescote will try to prevent by luring the heroes away to some amusement or to talk of another matter), they must wait outside for the phantom to appear the following night. The heroes are powerless to interact with the phantom, no matter what they do. It is an emotional impression left on the landscape, as unchangeable as a force of nature.

Exactly at the stroke of three in the morning, a glow will arise from the ground and resolve itself into the form of a beautiful young woman, clad in clothing fashionable a century ago. The colors are strangely bleached, so the actual color is indistinguishable. There is no sound to the entire scene, lending it an eerie quality.

The woman's hands are stained with something dark, and her dress is smeared as well. Abruptly, she whirls, a horrified expression on her face, and then turns and races toward the moors. Spilling forth from the abandoned kennels come the ghostly images of many hounds, each howling at their sighted prey. A man, also dressed in the fashions of a century ago, stands beside the open door of the kennel, pointing toward the fleeing form of the woman and crying out. When the last

of the hounds is gone, the grim-faced man races after them, his tricorn hat falling from his head.

Studying the man's face reveals an uncanny resemblance to Burton Wescote!

If the heroes follow the phantom hunt into the moors, they witness the events of what actually happened a century ago. How the final portion of this phantom scene plays out depends on the History the DM has chosen.

#1 or #3: Wescote might be carrying a rope, smirking over the girl's fate;

#2 or #4: or he might be casting about for a way to save her life.

Whichever the case, the heroes can determine the true villain by witnessing this. and the resting place of Ann. Unfortunately, the end of this little play results in the spontaneous creation of a pack of bog hounds who arise from the murky waters to attack. If any of the heroes attempt to interfere with this phantom scene, the Moor Hound arises as well, bounding out of the bog to bring death to the interlopers.

Bog Hounds (9): Int Semi; AL NE; AC 5; MV 15; HD 2+2; hp 12 each; THAC0 19; #AT 3; Dmg 1–4/1–4/1–6; SZ M; ML 15; XP 65 each.

The Moor Hound: Int Very; AL NE; AC 2; MV 18; HD 8; hp 64; THAC0 13; #AT 3; Dmg 1–6/1–6/1–8; SD Hit only by +1 or greater enchantment; MR 15%; SZ L; ML 20; XP 3,000.

If the heroes have been unable to identify the second figure in the phantom, Gabrielle will wait until they are well away from Wescote and then whisper, "Did he show you the apparition? All of it?" If the heroes press her for details, she informs them that there is another figure in the apparition, but that she has never, in her 30 years of service here, mustered the courage to venture out into the bog at night to identify it.

Regardless of whether the party saw the other figure, she tells them of the master's strange habit: He disappears into the bog every morning for about an hour. He comes back looking queasy and sick, and Gabrielle often hears him gagging later in the day.

he bog is not exceptionally large, but it houses a variety of creatures. Most of them can escape the danger the bog hounds pose, though some are simply able to defend themselves from the evil dogs. These encounters can take place any time the heroes are exploring the bog. However, more important than any denizen of the bog is the moors itself. Give a personality to the bog when the players ask for descriptions of their surroundings. The trees creak and groan with age, and the mires gasp and gurgle mournfully. Every breeze is a rotting breath, and every shadow shivers. Create character for the bog, and make the heroes feel as if they are being watched and threatened.

There are really only two encounters in this part of the adventure that can give the players information regarding the curse. The first is the clearing in which Ann's body lies; the second is the meeting with Ann. The other encounters simply add to the mystery and horror of the bog itself. Use these sparingly if the heroes are having difficulty, more liberally if they need a greater challenge.

The DM should review the rules for "Drowning In Quicksand" presented in Chapter 2 page 15 before proceeding.

A: Clearing

There is a sense of menace filling this clearing. It is larger than most of the dry patches in this bog and has several obvious patches of quicksand. Heavy undergrowth surrounds the clearing, obscuring anything that could be lurking there.

A small copse of trees huddles in the clearing, and a drone of insects fills the air. The stench of the bog is stronger and more horrible here. Mingling with the stink of vegetable rot is the unmistakable odor of an opened grave.

There is no encounter in this area unless the heroes begin digging in the quicksand. Then, the ghost of Ann Campbell does its best to distract the heroes from their task until she can either animate plants to drag the heroes toward the pool or create bog hounds, if it is dark. The Moor Hound itself will not appear unless night has fallen or the fog completely obscures the sun. See the next encounter for Ann's tactics should the heroes prove persistent in disturbing her body before bringing Wescote here.

This clearing is the site of the final encounter between Wescote and Campbell. The heroes may investigate this area as much as they like before the final encounter, but they find nothing of value.

B: The Two Faces of Ann Campbell

This encounter can occur on any trail in the bog. Once the heroes have completed some searching and after they have witnessed the phantom scene, Ann will appear to them. This is the ghost of Ann Campbell, not an animated corpse. She chooses to reveal herself once she realizes this is her best opportunity for peace.

When the heroes encounter Ann, they will see first a corrupted, moldering corpse. As they search the bog, have a randomly chosen hero make a Wisdom check. If the check succeeds, the hero has the feeling of malevolent eyes from behind staring at him. If the character whirls quickly, he sees a ghastly thing—a rotted head peering from the surface of the quagmire, staring intently at the party. Its mouth opens in a silent curse and the head sinks out of sight. This vision causes a horror check.

If the party investigates the quagmire, they will discover nothing. Ann's ghostly form has fled through the waters below the surface of the muck to avoid being spotted. If the characters actually begin poking around in the muck, Ann animates a vine or other plant to drive a character into the quicksand. A vine has a THAC0 of 15; if it hits, it wraps itself around a hero's leg or arm and begins pulling the character into the quicksand. The character must make a Strength check at –2 to avoid being pulled toward the swamp; two failed checks indicate the vine has succeeded in dragging the character below the surface. A hero drawn into the quicksand may continue to attack the vine at a –4 penalty, but only with a small weapon, like a knife or dagger. Larger weapons are useless in the muck. The vine can be severed by inflicting 10 hp of damage on it with a type P or S weapon.

The DM may substitute a harrying attack from another sort of plant such as a gnarled tree, flailing cattails, a thornbush, a spider plant, suffocating spanish moss and others.

After several encounters of this sort, Ann determines that the heroes intend to continue their investigation and appears to them.

> The clinging undergrowth at last parts on a dry blossom covered knoll. There stands a beautiful red-haired woman gathering flowers in the midst of the swamp. She looks up, unsurprised, and sets down her basket. She straightens, smoothing her old-fashioned dress, and waits for you to approach. Something about her features seems preternaturally calm.

If the heroes are observant, they may notice that this is the same woman whose portrait sits above Wescote's mantel. A successful Intelligence check indicates that "she looks familiar." If the heroes remark upon this resemblance, Ann tells the characters that she is a descendant of the Campbells they have heard about, come back to spread the truth about the night Ann was murdered.

Regardless of what the heroes say, Ann asks decides to tell the heroes a story. She tells them version #1 of the History, presenting herself as the innocent victim and Wescote as the villain. She omits the names of those involved in this little tale, but her outrage over the indignities she suffered mounts throughout the course of the story, until she is sobbing in rage at the end of the story.

If, at the end of this story, the heroes suggest that perhaps this woman is Ann Campbell, she acknowledges her identity. She says, "All I want is to be laid to rest. If I can but look upon the face of the man who caused my death, I can reconcile my spirit to its fate. If you could just find a way to bring him to the clearing in the northeast of this bog, I can at last find peace. From eve to morning's light is the only time that I can manifest fully. If you could bring him there then, I can calm the spirit of the swamp."

If the heroes suggest that she is being duplicitous, she flies into a rage, accusing the heroes of being Wescote's pawns, of wanting to see her suffer for eternity. Bog hound attacks on the heroes intensify when they leave Ann, until the heroes bring Wescote to the clearing. Nor will they permitted to leave the vicinity until the curse is broken.

If the heroes do not identify the woman as Ann Campbell, she remains calm. Even if the heroes are insulting, she keeps her temper under control. She asks that the heroes if they won't escort their host, Wescote to the northeast clearing so that she can speak to him about her "ancestor's" demise. She declines to go with them to Wescote's manor, saying that she won't feel comfortable in the house, and would rather meet with the lord someplace more neutral than his house. She requests that the characters bring him in the late afternoon or evening, so that Burton and Ann can both have the night to think on the words of the other. She does not seek vengeance, only to at last put the lord and this land at rest.

Once the heroes bring Burton to the northeast clearing during the hours of dusk and dawn, move to **Part V**, the climax.

C: Bog Hounds

This encounter takes place only at night or on exceptionally foggy days. While the heroes wander the morass of the bog, they hear the howling of the hounds nearby abruptly fall silent. For 1d10 rounds after the howling ceases, the hounds move stealthily to flank the heroes. All that may be discerned is the occasional panting of the hounds which halts just before someone can determine its source. When the party is surrounded, or when a hero straggles behind, the hounds leap in to the attack. This encounter does not occur if Ann has already persuaded the heroes to bring Wescote to the bog.

Bog Hounds (8): Int Semi; AL NE; AC 5; MV 15; HD 2+2; hp 10 each; THAC0 19; #AT 3; Dmg 1–4/1–4/1–6; SZ M; ML 15; XP 65 each.

D: Baby Shambler

This encounter is a place where the evil of a tragic death, and chance collided to create life. A shambling mound is growing created in this clearing, and it attacks anyone who enters. It won't pursue beyond the clearing's edge as its long roots form a tether. It is vulnerable to all forms of attack until fully grown, a process that will take three more weeks.

Shambling Mound (1): Int Low; AL N; AC 0; MV 6; HD 4; hp 24; THAC0 17; #AT 2; Dmg 2–8/2–8; SZ M; ML 15; XP 650.

This shambler entangles its victims if both of its arms hit. Entangled victims suffocate in 2–4 + Con hp bonus rounds unless the shambler is slain or the victim breaks free (on a successful bend bars/lift gates roll with a +20% bonus).

E: Wild Boars

This is a family of wild boars that has only recently wandered into the swamp. They have been harried by the bog hounds at night, and several of their number have been killed. This makes the rest of the boars much more protective of the remaining members of the family, and they charge intruders on sight. However, because the boars have been kept awake at night defending themselves from the hounds and are therefore extremely tired, any damage they cause is reduced by 1.

Boars (5): Int Semi; AL N; AC 7; MV 15; HD 3+3; hp 18, 14, 13, 12, 10; THAC0 17; #AT 1; Dmg 3–12; SZ S; ML 8; XP 175 each.

F: Snakes

This encounter can take place anywhere in the swamp, as snakes abound in the area. One snake might drop from a tree branch, or both might be disturbed by a careless hero's foot.

Snakes, Poisonous (2): Int animal; AL N; AC 6; MV 15; HD 2+1; hp 12, 8; THAC0 19; #AT 1; Dmg 1; SA Poison; SZ S; ML 8; XP 175 each.

Heroes bitten by the snakes must make a successful save versus poison or suffer 3 to 12 points of damage 1 to 6 rounds after the bite.

G: Shack

A small, crude hut stands on stilts at the edge of a pond. The house looks ready to collapse into the murky waters nearby. Smoke rises from the chimney.

If the heroes open the door to the shack, they must make a surprise check. Inside rest four corpses as if setting down to a meal. However, upon entering the cabin, the four zombies lurch to life and move toward the door to attack.

The zombies are the remnants of a hunting party. Trapped in the shack by the hounds, they eventually died of fear and horror. When their spirits left their bodies, the curse reanimated them and left them here for to attack any intruders.

Zombies (4): Int Non; AL N; AC 8; MV 6; HD 2; hp 14, 10, 10, 8; THAC0 19; #AT 1; Dmg 1–8; MR Special; SZ M; ML Special; XP 65 each.

here are four different endings based on the History the DM has chosen. The heroes should have discovered whether Burton is a murderer or a victim through earlier clues, though they may remain uncertain until the very end. Whatever the history, and regardless of Ann's and Burton's motives and alignments, the climax depends on the heroes agreeing to lead Wescote to Campbell for a face-to-face meeting, where they can discuss their differences—and where the Moor Hound can force the curse to its inevitable conclusion. When the heroes have managed to bring Burton to the site of Ann's death, read or paraphrase the following.

> The day has turned misty, the fog obscures the land. The day is unnaturally still as you set out from the manor into the bog. It is as though every living creature senses a coming storm and hides. There is an electric tension in the air, and you can't help but wonder when the storm is going to break.

In all four versions of this ending, the Moor Hound makes an appearance to attack the heroes. In all four versions, there are bog hounds standing ready when the meeting takes place, hidden in the brambles at the edge of the clearing. But, who they attack and how they attack are different according to each ending.

Bog Hounds (15): Int Semi; AL NE; AC 5; MV 15; HD 2+2; hp 14 each; THAC0 19; #AT 3; Dmg 1–4/1–4/1–6; SZ M; ML 15; XP 65 each.

The Moor Hound: Int Very; AL NE; AC 2, MV 18; HD 8; hp 64; THAC0 13; #AT 3; Dmg 1–6/1–6/ 1–8; SD Hit only by +1 or greater enchantment; MR 15%; SZ L; ML 20; XP 3,000.

Unless otherwise noted all elements of the meeting remain the same. In each ending, the two adversaries eye each other carefully, from across the clearing. Burton stands his ground warily, while Ann's ghostly form rises from the bog where her body lies.

After a few moments, they step forward to speak to each other, drawing near so that they can converse without others overhearing. The rest is outlined below.

#1 The Scoundrel: In this history, Wescote commands the Moor Hound, and is looking for a way to come to meet Campbell so that he can set the Moor Hound on her. With the party present, however, he must set the Moor Hound on them while he attempts to dispatch Campbell with a broad sword forged of silver, which he buckles on "for protection, in case of treachery" when the party leads him out to meet Campbell. He intends to break the curse by being rid of her and then disposing of the witnesses to his evil.

When the two meet, he interposes himself between the party and Campbell, so that they cannot see him preparing to draw the sword. Meanwhile, the Moor Hound comes up behind the party (assuming they are watching the meeting between the two), and as Burton draws his sword and begins to attack Campbell, the Moor Hound attacks the heroes.

The party has nine rounds to break free of the Moor Hound before Wescote kills Campbell. The Moor Hound, meanwhile, blocks the way to Campbell and attacks any who try to aid her. If several heroes go to her aid, the Moor Hound attacks the most powerful character. Once the heroes have entered the combat, Campbell can retreat and send in the bog hounds, who are waiting for her command. The bog hounds attack the Moor Hound, allowing the heroes to concentrate on Wescote.

As soon as Wescote falls, the mist breaks, allowing the sun to spill through. It casts its rays across the clearing, dispersing the bog hounds and leaving the Moor Hound standing. Whatever damage it has taken from the heroes and the bog hounds now becomes real damage, and it can be destroyed forever.

When both Wescote and the Moor Hound are vanquished, Campbell's ghost begins to fade. Her curse having run its course and her vengeance achieved, Ann is ready to rest. But first she turns to thank her rescuers.

Ann turns and smiles at you as the sun's rays gain force. She says, "I thank the powers that be for sending you to help break the curse. I have nothing with which to reward you, but you have my eternal gratitude." She smiles wryly. "For what that's worth." The sunbeams flow through her, and her form becomes more and more insubstantial, until she is gone altogether.

If Campbell is defeated, Wescote and the Moor Hound turn on the party. Though Campbell is destroyed, the presence of the Moor Hound keeps Wescote from aging. If the Moor Hound is killed (as it can be once Campbell is gone), Wescote ages suddenly, the century of youthfulness catching up to him. He withers and dies before the party's eyes. Even if the Moor Hound is not killed, Wescote wastes no breath in explaining himself to the heroes. He believes it is better to be rid of them quickly.

If he defeats the party, he continues on in his curst existence. The bog hounds can no longer be created, but the Moor Hound is still there to harass travelers and bring them to his door. Wescote's immortality is no longer dependent on drinking bog water, but he still cannot wander far from his house, so he lures travelers to his house, wrings them for news and comradery, killing them when he tires of them.

#2 The Shrew: Campbell says her fondest wish is for the "reconciliation" between the two. In reality, she was hoping to lure Wescote out on his own, but accepts the party's presence as the next best

thing. Once he has come before her, she appears in her beautiful guise, and approaches him as if to exchange whispers of times past. When the two have closed, she concentrates for a moment, and the Moor Hound comes charging into the clearing. It pauses and then turns and attacks the party, attempting to slay them all.

Meanwhile, the bog hounds hidden in the weeds nearby come charging out, barreling directly toward Wescote. Campbell retreats to hover over one of the bog patches so that she'll be harder to attack. She watches the battle in contentment, thinking it certain that her enemy will be defeated today.

During this, the fog has been fading. After three rounds, the sun breaks through for a moment, through a gap in the clouds and the fog, and strikes the Moor Hound. Now, with the beast actually vulnerable, the party can kill it. But they had better hurry, for Wescote can stand up to the bog hounds for only 10 rounds, three of which are already gone. As in #1, the Moor Hound moves to attack any hero who goes to his aid.

Campbell continues to watch the fracas, attacking only if the Moor Hound is reduced to 15 hp. She attacks the strongest character, or the one who seems most likely to cause her the greatest damage. If Wescote is killed, she laughs loudly and descends into the bog. She sends the Moor Hound away, leaving the heroes to bear Wescote's body back to the manor. She haunts the bog to harass travelers, until the Moor Hound is destroyed and her body is dredged from the mire and laid to rest.

If Campbell and the Moor Hound are destroyed, Wescote lets out a sigh of relief and slumps to the ground. Any bog hounds left alive crumple away to nothingness as their creator is destroyed. The sun breaks through the fog for good just as he hits the ground. Wescote lies there in the grass for a moment.

> Burton basks in the sun's rays for a moment, his eyes closed. Lacerations cover his body, testimony of the ferocity of the bog hounds'

> attacks. He breathes heavily for a few moments, and then rises to his feet. He smiles shakily at you, and says, "I owe you my life. For the first time in years, I feel like I actually have something to live for. For that alone, I am forever in your debt.
>
> "Please, come back to the manor to rest and healing. I'll do what I can to make sure you are amply rewarded."

That said, Wescote leads the way back to the manor to reward the heroes. He shows them to the room where he has been storing the wedding gifts and allows each hero to select one. Should the heroes ever travel this way again, they will be welcome at Wescote Manor.

#3 Evil Company: When both of the main players in this tragedy are evil, neither places any credence in the good will of the other. Both also suspect the heroes of secretly working with their enemy. Burton has brought a silver sword with which to kill the ghost.

The two have come to think enough alike that when they draw close together and see the heroes regarding them, they instantly assume the characters stand ready to attack. As one, the two rush the heroes and attack the party together for two rounds. The Moor Hound joins in as well, giving the party the fight of their life. When the two realize that they are both attacking the heroes, they turn on each other. The Moor Hound, however, continues to battle the party.

If the heroes drive the Moor Hound away and join in the battle, the tide turns in favor of the side they chose. Otherwise, Ann kills Burton in 12 rounds.

If the party sides with Wescote and destroys Campbell, the resolution continues as in #1. If the party sides with Campbell against Wescote, the adventure finishes as in #2. If they do nothing, Campbell kills Wescote, and it continues as in #2. Whatever their choice, the heroes will have to deal with the other once one of the two is destroyed.

#4 Curse of the Bog: In this history, the dog is the perpetuator of the curse, the linchpin that keeps the two from reconciling with one another. Its very existence depends on the two foes failing to discover that both or neither were at fault, depending on one's point of view. If the two meet and resolve their conflict, the Moor Hound's existence comes to an end. Therefore, the Hound works to ensure that such a reconciliation is never possible.

While the two meet, the Moor Hound silently destroys the bog hounds lurking in the weeds to ensure that they cannot be used against it in the coming battle. Since Campbell is not guiding the hounds, they offer no resistance to the Moor Hound. By the time the two are close enough to touch each other, the Moor Hound is ready for action. It crouches in the bushes at the edge of the clearing and readies its attack.

From where the heroes stand, they can see that the ghost's face is twisted with anger, but she is listening. Burton is speaking in a low, persuasive voice, too low for the heroes to hear. When he finishes explaining, he calls to the heroes to back him up, to tell what they saw during the phantom apparition.

Ann, her face more thoughtful, begins explaining her side of the story—and then the Moor Hound attacks, sensing that it is weakening. Ann and Burton are speaking to each other and do not see the Moor Hound coming. A surprise roll can be made for the heroes to keep it from attacking the two. If they fail, the Moor Hound falls upon Burton and tears at his throat. Ann stands back, aghast at the turn of events. If the heroes do nothing for two rounds, the Moor Hound rips out the throat of the man, and turns on the heroes, the curse finally made eternal.

If the heroes do step in, the reconciliation between the two suffers, as Burton suspects Ann of setting the Moor Hound on him. She must explain that she has nothing to do with the Moor Hound's movements, but to do this, she needs time. Only if the heroes can keep the Moor Hound from attacking the couple for 10 rounds can they ensure that the two placate each other's

hatred. If the Moor Hound escapes the party to attack Wescote, the process is set back again for at least another five rounds.

However, while the two are speaking reasonably to each other, the Moor Hound is completely vulnerable to ordinary weapons. It can be killed utterly if the two forgive each other. Breaking their concentration restores 15 hp to the Moor Hound, so its main efforts are devoted toward keeping the hatred between the two fanned. Once they have made peace, they stand back and watch the party destroy the Moor Hound. Only if the party members are in mortal danger do the two step in.

If the Moor Hound is killed, the curse is broken and the two can go to their rewards. Burton is able to live an ordinary existence; Ann finally gets to rest, her spirit appeased.

Burton gazes at the fading spirit of the ghost, once again beautiful. She smiles radiantly as she vanishes. Tears of joy stream down Burton's face as he turns to you.

"I thank you from the bottom of my heart," he says, "for you have granted peace both to myself and to Ann. I am forever in your debt." The sun bursts through the fog, as if to underscore the relief and happiness in Wescote's voice.

"I know that you are weary of battle, and probably more tired from the rest of your travails," he continues, "but I would be honored if you would help me to dredge out this morass to recover Ann's body, so that I may give it a real burial. I understand if you will not help, and I won't be affronted.

"Come, let's go back to the manor for a bath and some rest . . . and your reward." With a look over his shoulder, motioning for you to follow, he heads back to the house.

He will let the heroes select an item from the wedding gifts as a sign of gratitude. If they do not want to dredge for Ann's body, he will eventually send them on their way. He assures them that they'll always have a place to stay in Mordent if they ever return.

Burton Wescote

5th-level Human Warrior

S: 16   AL: LG or CE
D: 15   AC: 2
C: 15   Hps: 33
I: 14   THAC0: 16
W: 10   #AT: 1
Ch: 13 Dmg: 2d8
(broadsword)
MV: 12

Equipment: Wescote's house contains all manner of equipment. Most of it is old and of poor quality, because few supplies have reached the manor house since the curse began.

Description: Wescote is of medium height and slender frame, with tan skin, brown hair, and blue eyes. He wears spectacles, but his poor eyesight does not diminish his fighting capacity in any way. His slender build hides a strength one would not believe from his appearance. His manner is both confident and agitated at once, as though he were preoccupied.

Whatever history the DM chooses for the course of the adventure, Wescote is always charming and hospitable. His manner is pleasant and cultured, as befits a true gentleman. He will not offer violence to guests in his house unless provoked, even if the DM selects the evil version, unless he thinks he can get away with it.

He is hesitant to reveal his part in the disappearance of Ann Campbell. He does not want to admit that he played a significant part in it, whether or not he is guilty. He feels that it reflects badly on him, no matter the circumstances, and does his best to downplay his involvement, even going so far as to lie about the tale, if necessary.

Ann Campbell

7 HD Ghost

S: —   AL: CE
D: —   AC: 2
C: —   Hps: 53
I: 14   THAC0: 13
W: 12   #AT: 1
Ch: 15 Dmg: 1d8
MV: 12

Special Attacks: *Cause fear,* scarring (see below).
Special Defenses: Hit only by weapons of +1 or greater enchantment or of silver.

Equipment: Ann does not use equipment, preferring to attack hand-to-hand or to create her own weapons from the bog. She has the ability to *cause wounds* when she attacks. Every time she hits, there is a chance (1% per point of damage inflicted) that she has permanently scarred her victim. A scarred victim subtracts 1 point of Charisma. If the victim reaches 0 Charisma, the character dies.

Description: Though she was once surely beautiful, Ann Campbell's true form is now that of a ghastly creature, dripping quicksand and rotten flesh wherever she goes. With an effort, she can mask her spirit's deterioration, appearing as she did in life. When she first meets the party, she forces herself into her beautiful shape, so that she can distract them and give them information that they can trust.

Occasionally, while wandering through the bog, the heroes might witness her true, corrupted form regarding them from the safety of a quicksand morass. If they move to investigate her, she sinks beneath the surface and becomes incorporeal; thus rendering herself invisible.

Being dead has driven her insane. She now hates all life, Burton Wescote in particular. If possible, she manipulates the heroes into bringing him to the bog so that she can destroy him. Depending on the history chosen, however, she may reach a reconciliation with Wescote and be laid to rest.

Like Burton, she attempts to downplay her role in her death, painting herself as an innocent victim. No matter which history is chosen, she believes that she was the only one wronged, and it is nearly impossible to dissuade her.

She is tied to the bog and to her relationship with Burton, so Ann cannot pursue the heroes beyond the bog. However, she can send her hounds after them, up to a range of 10 miles.

She cannot *age* her opponents as can most ghosts. Instead, she works with her hounds, her scarring attack, and her ability to *cause fear* (save vs. paralyzation or flee for 1d6 rounds) to defend herself and to destroy those she hates.

Campbell's vulnerability is not only to magical and silver weapons, but also to the bites of real dogs. Normal dogs—but not the bog hounds or the Moor Hound itself—cause her twice normal damage. The Moor Hound may still attack Ann for normal damage, but the bog hounds are always under her control.

The Moor Hound

The Moor Hound, the main manifestation of the curse, is an enormous coal-black mastiff. Its eyes glow fiery red as though lit by a furnace, and its breath steams even in warm air. Its role in the adventure changes based on the history chosen. Once Campbell and Wescote meet face to face, the Moor Hound can no longer bound away once it has reached 0 hit points. Instead, it regenerates 1 point per turn, but it dies forever if reduced to 0 hit points. It cannot be harmed except by magical weapons, unless one of the effects noted below comes into play.

The Moor Hound is the protector of the curse, keeping it from ending. The arrival of the heroes may change everything. So the Moor Hound will do its best to make sure that the heroes do not break the curse, since its own existence depends on the continuation of the curse.

The Moor Hound cannot abide sunlight. If it is exposed to sunlight, even the briefest ray, it loses its invulnerability. This vulnerable state lasts for a number of days equal to the number of rounds the sun shone upon the Moor Hound. If sunlight falls on the Moor Hound for even part of one round, it is vulnerable for a day. If the sunlight touches the Moor Hound for three rounds, its vulnerability lasts three days.

The Moor Hound's master changes according to the history chosen by the DM.

In History #1, where Wescote is the villain and Campbell the innocent, the Moor Hound is under Wescote's control. Wescote uses the Moor Hound to attack Campbell and the heroes once they learn his secret.

In History #2, where Burton is innocent and Ann the villain, the Moor Hound is under Ann's control. Instead of attacking Burton herself, Ann uses the Moor Hound to wreak her vengeance. Only if the Moor Hound is losing a fight does she step in herself.

In History #3, where both Ann and Burton are evil, the Moor Hound is again under Ann Campbell's control. She uses it indiscriminately to attack the Wescote and the heroes. The Moor Hound prowls the night, seeking to kill whatever falls into its clutches.

In History #4, where the curse has come about as a misunderstanding, and where it is tied to a problem with the ancestors of the two, the Moor Hound is under no one's control. Instead, as the enforcer of the curse, it exists to prevent the two from reconciling. If the two do come to a reconciliation, the Moor Hound is weakened. Since it feeds on the hatred between the two, it loses some of its power should they reconcile. However, the hound will have stored enough hit points to remain a threat. It becomes a creature of 6 Hit Dice, 48 hit points, and Armor Class 4; and it loses its invulnerability to ordinary weapons.

BOG HOUND

	Bog Hounds	The Moor Hound
CLIMATE/TERRAIN:	Swamp	Swamp/Bog
FREQUENCY:	Very Rare	Unique
ORGANIZATION:	Pack	Pack Leader
ACTIVITY CYCLE:	Nocturnal	Nocturnal
DIET:	Carnivorous	Carnivorous
INTELLIGENCE:	Semi (3)	Very (12)
TREASURE:	None	None
ALIGNMENT:	Neutral evil	Neutral evil
NO. APPEARING:	2–20	1
ARMOR CLASS:	5	2
MOVEMENT:	15	18
HIT DICE:	2 + 2	8 (64 hp)
THAC0:	19	13
NO. OF ATTACKS:	3	3
DAMAGE/ATTACK:	1–4/1–4/1–6	1–6/1–6/1–8
SPECIAL ATTACKS:	Nil	None
SPECIAL DEFENSES:	Nil	Hit only by +1 or greater enchantment.
MAGIC RESISTANCE:	Nil	15%
SIZE:	M (6' long)	L (7' long)
MORALE:	Champion (15)	Fearless (20)
XP VALUE:	65 each	3,000

Bog hounds are large dogs, about the size of war dogs, created from the cursed bog by magic or the exceptionally strong will of a creature that can shape life. Sculpted of straw and mud, the hounds are granted life by wicked magic or a curse. Their color is a muddy brown, with splotches of yellow. The most frightening feature of these beasts is their lack of eyes: They have only empty black sockets to gaze out on the world.

Once the bog hounds are created, the Moor Hound leads them in whatever tasks their creator desires. The Moor Hound is made of the vapors of the bog rather than from mud and straw. It is a coal-black creature with flaming red eyes. Its jaws can easily fit around a full-grown man's head, and they are powerful enough to snap bone.

Though those that appear in this adventure are the creation of the curse of Ann Campbell on Burton Wescote, similar bog hounds and a leader Moor Hound can be used in any swampy area where a curse of magnitude has been laid.

Combat: Like ordinary dogs, the bog hounds attack by flanking their victims and closing to attack from all sides at once. When hunting, they send up an unearthly howl, subsiding only when they are about to close in. In combat, they react as ordinary hounds, unless the Moor Hound or their master instructs them to perform another task. When killed, they return to their original forms, dissolving into scattered straw and mud, a gasp of vapor escaping from the bodies.

The bog hounds are vulnerable to sunlight. If they are exposed to the sun, their supernatural essence evaporates like fog, and they become inanimate sculptures of straw and mud, trapped in the pose in which the light first caught them. These straw sculptures can be

destroyed by the slightest touch; unless extreme care is taken, the straw "statues" cannot be moved.

The Moor Hound can be hit only by enchanted weapons; however, it only *seems* to suffer real damage from them, for it can be destroyed only after it has been exposed to sunlight. Otherwise, once it has been reduced to 0 hit points or below, the Moor Hound bounds off to rejuvenate itself. It always leaves a trail of blood that leads directly to a pool of quicksand, but there is no further trace of the Moor Hound until the next night, when it comes back fully regenerated. If not exposed to sunlight, the Moor Hound cannot die. It can, however, be captured.

The Moor Hound is even more vulnerable to sunlight. If even the slightest beam directly hits the Moor Hound, it can be hit by ordinary weapons and permanently killed, breaking part of the curse which gave it life. Any "false" damage it took before being exposed to sunlight suddenly becomes real, perhaps slaying the Moor Hound outright. When the beast dies, a ghostly howling marks its passage into nothingness.

Habitat/Society: The bog hounds are under the control of the being who brought them to life. They have no other social order except that they follow the Moor Hound, who also serves the master of the bog hounds.

Ecology: As supernatural creatures, the Moor Hound and its minions have no place in any natural ecology. The bog hound's diet is listed as carnivorous. In truth, it needs to eat nothing; but when it attacks, it savages and devours only living, fleshy creatures. It gains no sustenance from eating—it is simply vicious.